A NOTE TO PARENTS

When your children are ready to "step into reading," giving them the right books—and lots of them—is as crucial as giving them the right food to eat. **Step into Reading Books** present exciting stories and information reinforced with lively, colorful illustrations that make learning to read fun, satisfying, and worthwhile. They are priced so that acquiring an entire library of them is affordable. And they are beginning readers with an important difference—they're written on four levels.

Step 1 Books, with their very large type and extremely simple vocabulary, have been created for the very youngest readers. **Step 2 Books** are both longer and slightly more difficult. **Step 3 Books,** written to mid-second-grade reading levels, are for the child who has acquired even greater reading skills. **Step 4 Books** offer exciting nonfiction for the increasingly proficient reader.

Children develop at different ages. **Step into Reading Books,** with their four levels of reading, are designed to help children become good—and interested—readers *faster*. The grade levels assigned to the four steps—preschool through grade 1 for Step 1, grades 1 through 3 for Step 2, grades 2 and 3 for Step 3, and grades 2 through 4 for Step 4—are intended only as guides. Some children move through all four steps very rapidly; others climb the steps over a period of several years. These books will help your child "step into reading" in style!

Text copyright © 1995 by Annabelle Prager. Illustrations copyright © 1995 by Marilyn Mets.
All rights reserved under International and Pan-American Copyright Conventions. Published in
the United States by Random House, Inc., New York, and simultaneously in Canada by Random
House of Canada Limited, Toronto.

Library of Congress Cataloging-in-Publication Data
Prager, Annabelle. The baseball birthday party / by Annabelle Prager ; illustrated by Marilyn Mets.
  p. cm. — (Step into reading. A step 2 book)
SUMMARY: Billy decides to have a party to show the other kids that he can play baseball, but his young
helper's mistake almost spoils the plan.
ISBN 0-679-84171-7 (pbk.) — ISBN 0-679-94171-1 (lib. bdg.)
[1. Baseball—Fiction. 2. Parties—Fiction.] I. Mets, Marilyn, ill. II. Title. III.
Series: Step into reading. Step 2 book.   PZ7.P8864Bas 1994   [E]—dc20 93-25258

Manufactured in the United States of America   10 9 8 7 6 5 4 3 2 1

STEP INTO READING is a trademark of Random House, Inc.

Step into Reading™

THE BASEBALL BIRTHDAY PARTY

By Annabelle Prager

Illustrated by Marilyn Mets

A Step 2 Book

Random House 🏠 New York

CHAPTER ONE

The new kid, Billy, stood

all by himself

way out in the field,

watching Nicky pitch the ball.

"I wish someone would

hit the ball out here,"

Billy said to himself.

"I could show Nicky and the other kids

how good I am.

They've never seen me play before."

Crack!

The girl at bat

gave the ball a smack.

It bounded along the ground

right to Billy.

"Here's my chance!" Billy shouted.

He held out his hands.

But the ball bounced under his glove,

through his legs,

and into a clump of grass.

"Get it! Get it!"

shouted Ann and Suzanne.

"Hurry! Hurry!"

shouted Denny and Dan.

Billy whirled around

so fast that—

boom!—

down he went,

right on top of the ball.

"Throw it to me!"

"Throw it here!"

"Throw it home!"

Voices shouted to him from all sides.

It was too late.

A runner slid across home plate.

Another one followed.

"We won! We won!"

shouted the other team.

Nicky threw his glove on the ground.

"We were one run ahead

till I put that new kid in the game,"

he said in a loud voice

to his pal Albert.

"Yeah," said Albert.

"We lost the game

because of him."

They walked off the field together.

CHAPTER TWO

Billy stayed on the ground

where he was.

"It's not fair," he cried.

He felt a little tap on his head.

"What's not fair?" said Dan.

"Nicky didn't put me in the game

till the last minute," said Billy.

"Then I blew it. Now everybody thinks

I'm a bad player.

They'll never ask me to play again."

"Nobody ever asks me to play either,"

said Dan.

"They always say,

'Sure you can play in our game...

next year.'"

"That's because you're such a little guy,"

said Billy.

"I'm new around here," said Billy.

"Nobody knows I can hit a home run

anytime I want."

"Anytime?" said Dan.

"Well, *almost* anytime," said Billy.

"Now nobody will ever know about it."

He put his head in his hands.

Suddenly, he sat up straight.

"I've got it!" he cried.

"Got what?" asked Dan.

"My birthday is coming," said Billy.

"I'll have a baseball birthday party

in my own backyard.

I'll hit a million billion home runs

for everybody to see."

"I want to come," said Dan.

"I love parties."

"Everybody loves parties," said Billy.

"I bet everybody will want to come.

EVERYBODY."

PARTY
Nicky
Albert
Ann
Suzanne
Morris

CHAPTER THREE

So Billy decided to have

a baseball birthday party

the very next Friday at three o'clock.

"Can I be your helper?" asked Dan.

"Why not?" said Billy.

"First we have to make invitations."

"I don't read and write

very well yet," said Dan.

"I'll do the writing," said Billy.

"You can do the mailing."

"Who are you going to invite?"

asked Dan.

"Let's see," said Billy.

"There's Nicky and Albert

and Ann and Suzanne.

There's Morris and Doris

and Denny…"

"…and Dan!" shouted Dan.

"That's me. Don't forget,

you're going to ask me."

"I know, I know," said Billy.

"Won't everybody be surprised

when I hit my home runs?"

Dan helped Billy put the invitations

in a shopping bag.

"Now take them

to the letter box on the corner,"

said Billy.

"Drop them in the slot."

"Shall I mail the bag too?"

asked Dan.

"No, silly," said Billy.

Dan walked down the street

till he came to a big box

with a slot in it.

He stuffed the invitations

through the slot.

"What a good helper I am," he said,

feeling very pleased with himself.

CHAPTER FOUR

On Monday,

Billy went to the school library.

He found a book called

Baseball Tips for Boys and Girls.

Every day he looked for tips…like

"If a ball bounds to you

along the ground,

keep your hands low,

fall to one knee, and

block it."

He found good tips for Dan too...like
"You'll never learn

to catch a ball

if you keep your eyes shut."

Every day they looked

in Billy's mailbox.

"Nothing yet," Billy would say.

By Wednesday,

there were still no answers.

"Are you sure you mailed

the invitations?" Billy asked Dan.

"Sure I'm sure," said Dan.

"Maybe everybody will call instead."

But the phone didn't ring.

Billy began to get worried.

"Tell you what," he said.

"You're my helper.

How would you like to play detective?"

"How do I do that?" asked Dan.

"Snoop around," said Billy.

"Find out who is coming to my party.

But don't say it's me

who wants to know."

CHAPTER FIVE

So Detective Dan set out

for the schoolyard.

Ann and Suzanne were playing

hopscotch.

"Did you get an invitation

for this Friday?"

Dan asked Suzanne.

"'Course I did," said Suzanne.

"I can't wait to see the lion."

"Wow!" said Dan.

"Billy didn't tell me

there was going to be a lion."

"They always have a lion at the circus,"

said Suzanne.

"You mean there's going to be

a circus too?" said Dan.

"Poor little Dan," said Ann.

"Don't you know there's going to be
a circus in Pottsville on Friday?"

"Why didn't you tell Billy about it?"
said Dan.

"Why should I tell Billy about it?"
asked Ann.

But Dan was already on his way

to see Nicky and Albert.

Dan tugged on Nicky's sleeve.

"Who is coming to the baseball party?"

he asked.

"What baseball party?" said Nicky.

"The one that Billy is having

at three o'clock on Friday,"

said Dan.

Nicky gave Albert a funny look.

"You mean that butterfingers

who can't catch a ball?" he said.

"How should I know?"

Dan walked back to Billy's house
feeling mad.

"How did it go?" cried Billy.

"I don't want to be a detective,"
said Dan.

"It's not nice at all."

"I guess I shouldn't have asked

such a little guy to take on

such a big job," said Billy.

He began to get very, very worried.

"Back where I used to live,

people always answered invitations,"

he said.

"Maybe around here

they just show up."

CHAPTER SIX

Friday was a beautiful day for baseball.

Dan went to Billy's house

to help him get ready for the party.

They put out big bowls of popcorn,

pitchers of iced lemonade,

and blue and red balloons that said

"I love baseball."

Best of all was

the big gooey chocolate cake

with candles on it.

Then they sat on the porch steps
to wait for the first guest.
They waited and waited,
but nobody came.
"It's a quarter past three,"
said Billy.
"I guess people around here
don't like to come
to parties on time."
They waited some more.
It got to be three-thirty,
then a quarter to four.
Still nobody came.

"I guess people around here

don't like to come to parties at all!"

yelled Billy.

"I'm going back where I used to live."

He ran into his house

and slammed the door.

CHAPTER SEVEN

Dan didn't know what to do.

So he grabbed two fistfuls of popcorn

and started down the street

for home.

He hadn't gone far when

who should he bump into

but Nicky and Albert.

"Why are you so late?" he cried.

"Late for what?" said Albert.

"We were just going to walk by
   that new boy's house
   to see who he invited to his dumb party.
   We're mad because he didn't invite us,"
   said Nicky.

"He did invite you," said Dan.

"He invited EVERYBODY.
   I mailed the invitations my very self,
   in that letter box over there."

"That's not a letter box,"
   said Albert.

"It is so," said Dan.

"See, it says LETTER on it."

"It says LITTER on it," said Nicky.

"Litter means 'Garbage.'
You mailed the invitations
in a garbage can!"

CHAPTER EIGHT

"There's a party going on!"

shouted Albert.

"And nobody's at it!"

"We have to tell everybody right away!"

cried Nicky.

So Albert and Nicky started

up the street yelling,

"Party at Billy's house!"

"What can I do?" said Dan.

"Go tell Billy that we're all

on our way!" shouted Nicky.

Dan dashed to Billy's house.

"Stop packing!" he yelled.

"Everybody's coming!

EVERYBODY!"

CHAPTER NINE

Sure enough,

in no time at all,

Billy's yard was full of people.

None were happier to be there

than Albert and Nicky.

"This is awesome," Nicky said to Billy.

"We thought you didn't want us

at your party

because we were sore losers!"

"No kidding?" said Billy.

"And I thought nobody wanted to come
because I messed up the game."

"Hey, anyone can miss a ball,"
said Albert.

"Nicky does it all the time."

"I do not!" shouted Nicky.

"You'll see."

CHAPTER TEN

So Billy's party turned out

to be a great party,

even though it was a late party.

They ate up all the popcorn,

drank down all the iced lemonade,

and when the last crumb of gooey cake

was gone,

they chose up sides

and played baseball.

Everybody got to play,

even Dan.

Nobody missed the ball...*too* often.
And everybody was surprised
when a hard ball bounded
along the ground to Billy.
He kept his hands low,
fell to one knee,
and blocked it.

They were even more surprised
when Morris threw the ball to Dan.
He kept his eyes open and caught it.

But the biggest surprise of all came

when the score was tied

six to six

and Billy came up to bat one last time.

He hit the ball

so hard and so far

it took five minutes to find it

in the neighbor's

holly bush!

"This party was a neat idea,"

said Nicky.

"We've found a great new player!"

"And who will ever forget

the invitations that got mailed

in a garbage can?"

said Albert.

"Hooray for Billy!"

shouted Ann and Suzanne

and Morris and Doris

and Denny...

"...and Dan!" shouted Dan.

"Don't forget hooray for me,

'cause I'm the one who did it."